The Adventures

By Ocean Ramsey

Photographs by Juan Oliphant

Illustrations by Taylor Cunningham

This book is dedicated to my wonderful mother, who for many years, encouraged me to write a children's book based around my real-life experiences.

Thank you to my dear parents for raising me to care for other species of animals, to respect nature, and to explore.

-Ocean Ramsey (Author)

Juan is a boy who grew up in Hawaii. Juan's parents taught him how to swim, freedive, and surf in the big waves on the north shore of the island of O'ahu. One day Juan was on the beach in front of his house and saw a shadow near the shore. It was big!

Juan grabbed his mask, snorkel, and fins and took a look underwater. He saw a shark wrapped up in a net, weak and barely struggling; he could tell it would die if he didn't help it.

Juan called to his friend Moana who was on the beach. "Help, there is a shark wrapped up in a net!" Moana got her dad, and they came over to help Juan and the shark.

Moana's dad used a tool and carefully cut the net off of the shark and they all watched as it slowly swam away. They saved the shark's life and they were so happy!

The next day Juan and
Moana went to the
beach. While they were
snorkeling, the big shark
came back. She swam
under Juan and Moana
and said, "Mahalo
(which means "thank
you" in Hawaiian
language) for saving my
life!"

The shark said, "My name is Curly Girl because
my dorsal fin is curled over. Follow me, and I
will show you the best dive spots."

Juan and Moana were so happy Curly Girl was
alive, they held hands and followed Curly Girl.

As they swam, Curly girl said she sensed something, so they followed her special shark-senses to find a sea turtle wrapped up in fishing line.

The fishing line was cutting the turtle's fins and neck. Juan and Moana had brought a special diver cutting tool. Moana carefully and quickly cut the fishing line off the sea turtle.

When the sea turtle was free, she said, "Mahalo for saving my life! My name is Alexis, I was trying to eat the seaweed, but I didn't realize it was growing on fishing line that was left on the reef."

"The more I struggled and tried to use my flippers to wipe it off the more I became wrapped up."

Alexis thanked Curly Girl, Juan, and Moana and told them about a beautiful secret cave nearby with the special Hawaiian sunrise shells in it. So they all started to follow Alexis to the cave.

On the way to the cave, they saw a pod of dolphins. They noticed one looked different and was struggling to keep up.

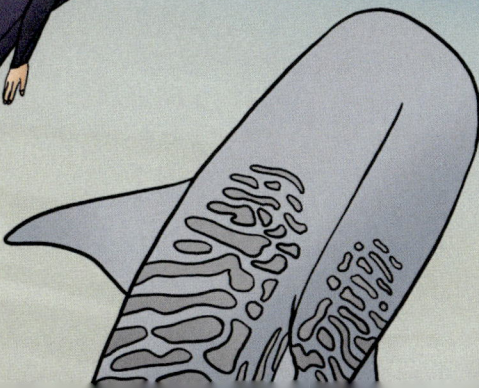

There was something stuck on its tail! They stopped and realized that the baby dolphin had a plastic bag wrapped around it!

Moana dove down as the pod swam by and twirled around, hoping the baby dolphin would be curious and come over.

It worked! The baby dolphin came close, and Juan got the plastic bag off of the dolphin's tail.

Oh mahalo! My name is Chiara, and my baby Natalie was getting so tired from dragging that thing around. Natalie thought it was a leaf, and she got wrapped up while playing with it. She was getting weaker every day. You saved her life! The bag came from that giant boat with all the hooks.

Juan, Moana, Curly Girl, and Alexis swam over to the boat to return the bag and ask them nicely not to pollute. As they got closer, they were shocked to see a Galapagos shark, Sandbar shark, and Hammerhead shark swimming in circles; they were all caught on hooks and lines and couldn't get free. Moana dove down and carefully cut all the lines short.

"Thank you for saving us!" The beautiful Galapagos shark said, "we were getting hurt and having a hard time breathing because we couldn't swim properly. My name is Taylor, and these are my friends Tracy and Andriana."

Tracy said, "Thank you! The line was cutting into my gills, fins, and scratched my eye, and Andriana might've broken part of her jaw while trying to get free."

That boat is devastating! How can that be legal? Moana wondered. The boat drove away before they could talk to them.

Their new shark friends thanked them again and then swam off to do their important job keeping the reef and other animal populations healthy.

Juan said, "I will reuse the bag for art, and we will ask our parents about that kind of big fishing boat tonight. Let's go to the cave."

As they swam towards the cave, they saw something HUGE near the surface. It was wriggling and covered in spots. "Ooooooooohh, my stomach," the spotted figure wailed. Suddenly it burped up a bunch of shiny candy wrappers and plastic bottle caps!

"Oh no! You're not supposed to eat wrappers and plastic!" Juan said.

The giant made a sad face and explained he didn't mean to but that they were floating where he was filter-feeding.

"I am so big, so I can't see what I am eating, and now I always feel sick. Why is there so much debris (garbage) in the water now?" The giant asked. Juan and Moana looked at each other with a frown because they knew humans were to blame. They promised to clean up the beaches and waterways and to help teach others not to pollute.

Juan apologized that there was trash in the water, and then he asked the giant politely, "If you don't mind me asking, what are you?"

"My name is Thomas, and I am a whale shark, the largest shark in the ocean. I am a gentle filter feeder, but my kind is disappearing. Thank you for telling everyone back on land to stop polluting and to please be nicer to sharks." Thomas said with a worried tone as he glided away.

Juan, Moana, and Curly Girl followed Alexis into the secret cave

The cave was incredible and filled with beautiful corals and special Hawaiian sunrise shells.

The current was getting stronger, and Moana was starting to get cold, so they thanked Alexis and Curly Girl for taking them to the cave and said they would head back to shore.

Curly Girl said she would escort them back to shore and look out for them as their ʻaumākua because they had saved her. Moana and Juan said they were honored and grateful and would look out for Curly girl as ohana (family.)

On their way back to the beach, they swam over beautiful healthy corals. However, as they got closer to shore, the corals were increasingly grey and white and looked more like a graveyard. Soon there were no fish in sight.

The water near shore was murky and smelled bad. They noticed a drain and dirty water coming out.

They popped their heads out of the water and saw an auntie on the beach. "Aloha, excuse me, auntie, do you know what this black water is from?" Moana asked. "Aloha dear, my name is Grandma Marlu, and that pollution is coming from those industrial buildings over there."

"They burn things for energy and make cleaning and paint chemicals. We need to stop them from polluting and killing the reef here. Maybe you two could take underwater photos and help show people, and those companies, the reef and fish are dying because of this." Grandma Marlu suggested.

Moana also asked, "Grandma Marlu, we also saved some sharks from a HUGE boat that had thousands of fishing hooks. They must kill so many marine animals! How can that be legal?"

"Yes, it's very sad, those industrial-scale, commercial fishing boat fleets put out hundreds of miles of baited hooks and kill so many different animals. They take so many fish away from the marine animals, and that also takes fish away from local single-line fisherman. You should get photos and tell people to vote to limit or stop them." Said Grandma Marlu. Juan and Moana thanked her and started to walk home.

As they walked home, they heard someone yelling their names, "Juan and Moana!" It was their friendly neighbor, Shiloh. "I think a manta ray just got accidentally caught on my single fishing line. I don't want it to get hurt."

"I don't want to stress it out more by pulling it in to cut the line off. Can you two swim out and cut the line short?" Shiloh asked nicely. He was worried for the manta ray.

"Thank you for letting us know we would love to help," said Juan, and they rushed into the water to cut the line as short as possible. The manta ray was named Blake, and he was so happy to be free.

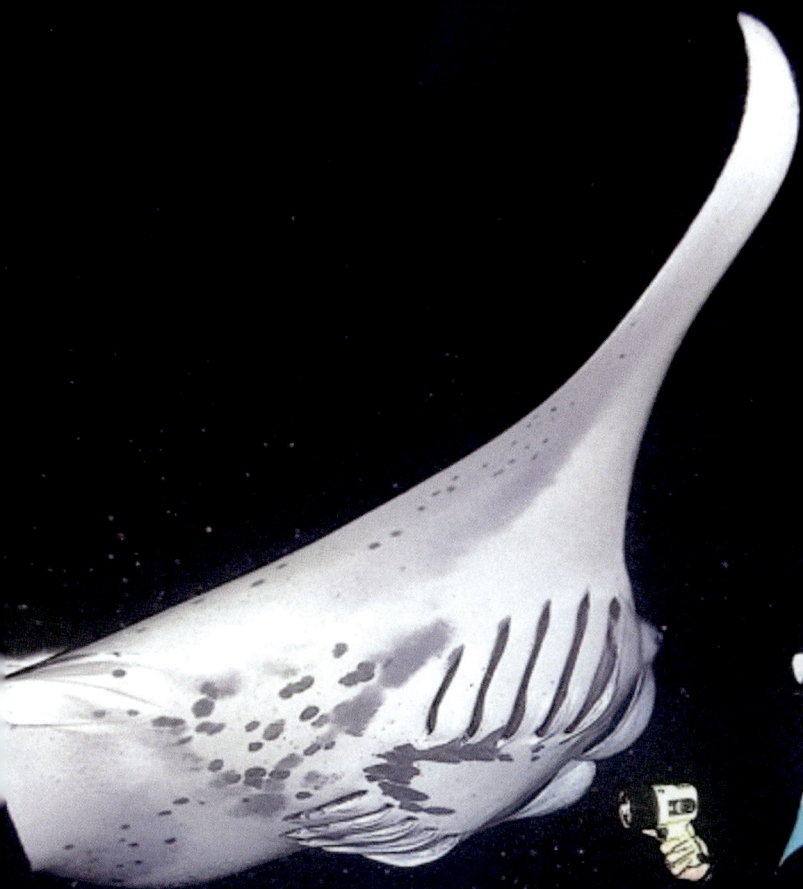

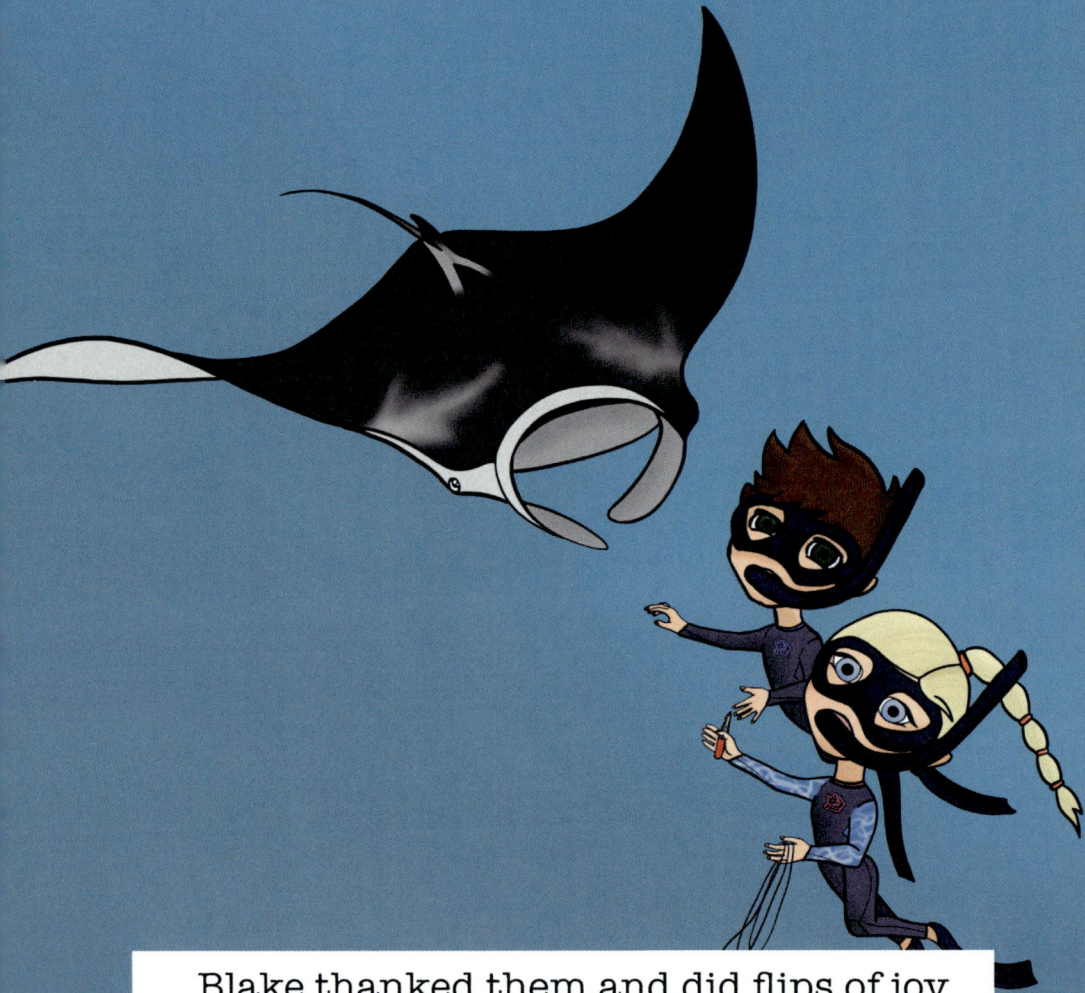

Blake thanked them and did flips of joy
before he swam off. Juan and Moana
knew it was important that they had cut
the line fast and as short as possible so
Blake wouldn't get wrapped whenever he
did flips. "I am so happy our local
fisherman friend Shiloh asked us to help,"
Juan said as they swam back to shore.

Shiloh, their fisherman friend, thanked them for helping and explained he doesn't like to leave the fishing line on the reef. He said he always cuts the line fast, and short, if he accidentally catches something besides his dinner. He told them it hurts his future fishing if a lot of fishing line is left on the reef, or if many other important animals are entangled, eventually the whole ecosystem suffers.

Moana and Juan made it home and told their parents about their adventures. Their parents liked the idea of having them photograph and share their stories to inspire others to make changes, to save the reef, to do beach clean up's, and to help look for entangled animals.

So Juan "Shark boy" and Ocean girl still work every day to help save marine animals and the reef. They take photos to share stories to inspire people to help save and protect the beautiful and important marine life in the ocean.

A real photo of Ocean Ramsey with "Grandma Great White." Photo taken by Juan Oliphant in 2019, off their home on O'ahu.

Join Shark Boy & Ocean Girl by helping to teach others about marine conservation.

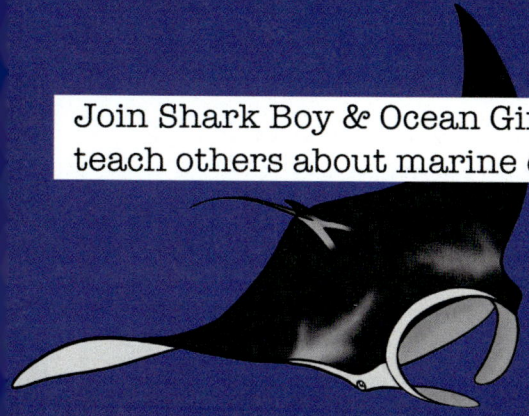

Help protect nature by reducing energy use, preventing marine debris, and picking up debris anytime you see it.

Don't eat seafood from industrial fishing fleets and try to eat more plant -based to help save all animals.

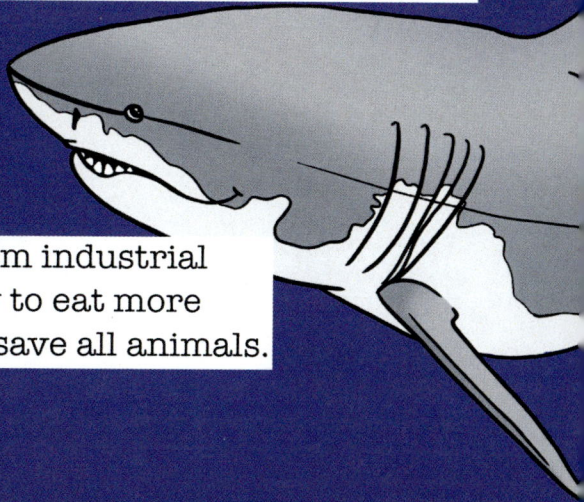

SAVE THE SEA TURTLES INTERNATIONAL
ONE OCEAN CONSERVATION
& WATER INSPIRED

Thank you for helping Juan and Ocean girl save the ocean. The proceeds from this book go to Save The Sea Turtles International nonprofit and One Ocean Conservation. Save The Sea Turtles International was founded by Juan's mother, Marlu Oliphant, in 1988 and is now led by Juan Oliphant and his wife, Ocean Ramsey (Moana means Ocean in the Hawaiian language.) They co-founded One Ocean Conservation and work daily cutting the fishing line off of sharks, sea turtles, and the reef. They take photos of marine conservation issues to use when speaking up for marine life, educating others, and pushing for changes for better protection for marine life. Mahalo nui loa (thank you so much.)
Learn more at OneOceanDiving.Com

Learn more and get involved at

OceanRamsey.Org

&

OneOceanDiving.Com

Made in the USA
Monee, IL
22 November 2020